LULLABIES
AND BABY SONGS

JANNAT MESSENGER

DIAL BOOKS FOR YOUNG READERS
•
NEW YORK

·   *To all my babies*   ·

First published in the United States 1988 by
Dial Books for Young Readers
A Division of NAL Penguin Inc.
2 Park Avenue
New York, New York 10016
Published in Great Britain by
William Heinemann Ltd
Pictures copyright © 1988 by Jannat Messenger
Compilation copyright © 1988 William Heinemann Ltd
All rights reserved
Printed in Great Britain by the Springbourne Press Ltd.
First edition
O B E
2 4 6 8 10 9 7 5 3 1

Library of Congress Cataloging in Publication Data
Messenger, Jannat. Lullabies and baby songs.
Summary: An illustrated collection of
eleven lullabies from a variety of sources.
1. Lullabies, American. 2. Children's poetry, American.
3. Sleep—Juvenile poetry. [1. Lullabies.
2. Poetry—Collections. 3. Sleep—Poetry] I. Title.
PS3563.E812L8 1988   821′.008′09282   87-15590
ISBN 0-8037-0491-7

· CONTENTS ·

· GOLDEN SLUMBERS ·

Golden slumbers kiss your eyes,
Smiles awake you when you rise.
Sleep, pretty baby, do not cry,
    And I will sing a lullaby.
    And I will sing a lullaby.

Care is heavy, therefore sleep you;
You are care, and care must keep you.
Sleep, pretty baby, do not cry,
    And I will sing a lullaby.
    And I will sing a lullaby.

· HE MADE FOR ME A LOVE TOKEN ·

He made for me a love token,
Cress, sorrel, the gypsy weaver,
A crown of willow ne'er to be broken,
    Cress, sorrel, and samphire.
He wove a white square to be my pillow,
A fine green cradle of the green willow.
But Cromwell sent him o'er the billow,
    Cress, sorrel, and samphire.

· THE CRADLE IS WARM ·

The cradle is warm and there shall you sleep,
    Safe and warm, little baby,
Angels shall come and stand closely to keep,
    Watch over you, little baby,
Bye-bye now, go to sleep,
    So sweetly to sleep, little baby.

· DANCE TO YOUR DADDY ·

Dance to your daddy,
  My little babby,
Dance to your daddy,
  My little lamb.

You shall have a fishy
  In a little dishy,
You shall have a fishy
  When the boat comes in.

· SLEEP, BABY, SLEEP ·

Sleep, baby, sleep!
Our cottage vale is deep,
The little lamb is on the green,
With snowy fleece so soft and clean,
    Sleep, baby, sleep.

Sleep, baby, sleep!
I would not, would not weep;
The little lamb he never cries,
And bright and happy are his eyes,
    Sleep, baby, sleep!

Sleep, baby, sleep!
Thy rest shall angels keep;
While on the grass, the lamb shall feed
And never suffer want or need,
    Sleep, baby, sleep.

· ALL THE PRETTY LITTLE HORSES ·

Hush-a-bye, hush-a-bye,
Go to sleepy, little baby,
When you are awake, you will have cake,
And all the pretty little horses.
Black and bay, dapple and gray
Coach and six-a little horses.

Way down yonder
Down in the meadow,
There's a poor little lammie.
The bees and the butterflies,
Buzzing round its eyes,
The poor little thing cries Mammy.

Hush-a-bye, don't you cry,
Go to sleepy, little baby,
When you awake, you will have cake,
And all the pretty little horses.

· SLEEP MY BABY ·

Sleep my baby, sleep my darling,
　Baby lullaby,
On your cradle moon is shining
　Softly from the sky.

I shall sing and tell you stories,
　If you close your eyes,
Slumber quietly while I lull you,
　Baby lullaby.

· THE ROCKING CAROL ·

Little Jesus, sweetly sleep, do not stir;
We will lend a coat of fur,
   We will rock you, rock you, rock you,
   We will rock you, rock you, rock you;
See the fur to keep you warm,
Snugly round your tiny form.

Mary's little baby, sleep, sweetly sleep.
Sleep in comfort, slumber deep;
   We will rock you, rock you, rock you,
   We will rock you, rock you, rock you;
We will serve you all we can,
Darling, darling, little man.

· HOW MANY MILES TO BABYLON ·

How many miles to Babylon?
Three score and ten.
Can I get there by candlelight?
Yes, and back again.
If your heels are nimble and light,
You may get there by candlelight.

· A WELSH LULLABY ·

Lullaby, my pretty one,
Gone the day and set the sun,
Lullaby, my pretty one,
   And sleep until the morning,
   And sleep until the morning.

Little one, now take thy rest
Like the birdie in its nest,
Little one, now take thy rest,
   And sleep until the morning,
   And sleep until the morning.

Lullaby, my dearest one,
Sleep for now thy play is done.
Lullaby, my dearest one,
   And sleep until the morning,
   And sleep until the morning.

Go to bed first,
A golden purse;
Go to bed second,
A golden pheasant;
Go to bed third,
A golden bird.